Nighty Night, Sleepy Sleeps

BRIAN ANDERSON

A NEAL PORTER BOOK
ROARING BROOK PRESS
NEW YORK

To Mom and Dad, for the sacrifices and the love and letting me draw all the time.
To Tammy, for more things than can be listed here.
To Liam and Sophie, who make all this stuff up.
And Rosemary and Neal for the opportunity.

Copyright © 2008 by Brian Anderson

A Neal Porter Book

Published by Roaring Brook Press

Roaring Brook Press is a division of Holtzbrinck Publishing Holdings Limited Partnership

175 Fifth Avenue, New York, New York 10010

All rights reserved

www.roaringbrookpress.com

Distributed in Canada by H. B. Fenn and Company, Ltd.

Library of Congress Cataloging-in-Publication Data

Anderson, Brian, (Brian Calvin), 1974-

Nighty night, sleepy sleeps / Brian Anderson. — 1st ed.

p. cm.

"A Neal Porter book."

Summary: Doug and Sophie, from the comic strip "Dog eat Doug," share all sorts of exploits to avoid going to bed.

ISBN-13: 978-1-59643-356-4   ISBN-10: 1-59643-356-6

[1. Stories in rhyme. 2. Bedtime—Fiction. 3. Babies—Fiction. 4. Dogs—Fiction.] I. Anderson, Brian, (Brian Calvin), 1974- Dog eat Doug. II. Title.

PZ8.3.A5442Nig 2008   [E]—dc22   2008007505

Roaring Brook Press books are available for special promotions and premiums.

For details, contact: Director of Special Markets, Holtzbrinck Publishers.

Printed in China

First edition October 2008

2   4   6   8   10   9   7   5   3   1

Up the stairs.

Down the stairs.

Through the laundry.

Chew

the

laundry.

No time for
nighty night,
sleepy sleeps.

Time
to
hide.

Daddy's
shoes.

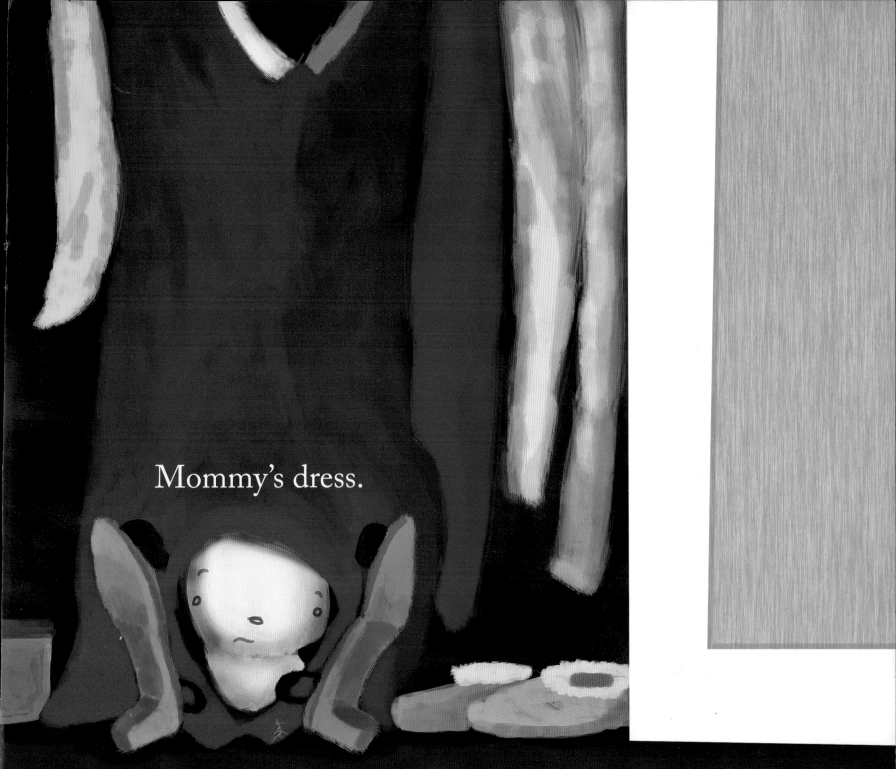

Mommy's dress.

Run around.
Make a **mess**.

No time for
nighty night,
sleepy sleeps.

In the closet,
still and quiet.
When Mom
finds us . . .

Now the cupboards. Pots and pans.

Too
much
noise.

CLANG!

BANG!

BAM!

Dive under the couch.

Dusty and
c r e e p y.

We're bumped and bruised,
but **far** from sleepy.

No time for
nighty night,
sleepy sleeps.

Bark like you are

SAD.

AAROOOOOOOO

Cry like you are

MAD.

Climb
the
clock.
Can't
tell
time.

That's okay . . .

We'll stay up till twelve o'nine!

Down
to the
basement,
not one lamp.

Bad idea.

Dark
and
damp!

No time for
nighty night,
sleepy sleeps.

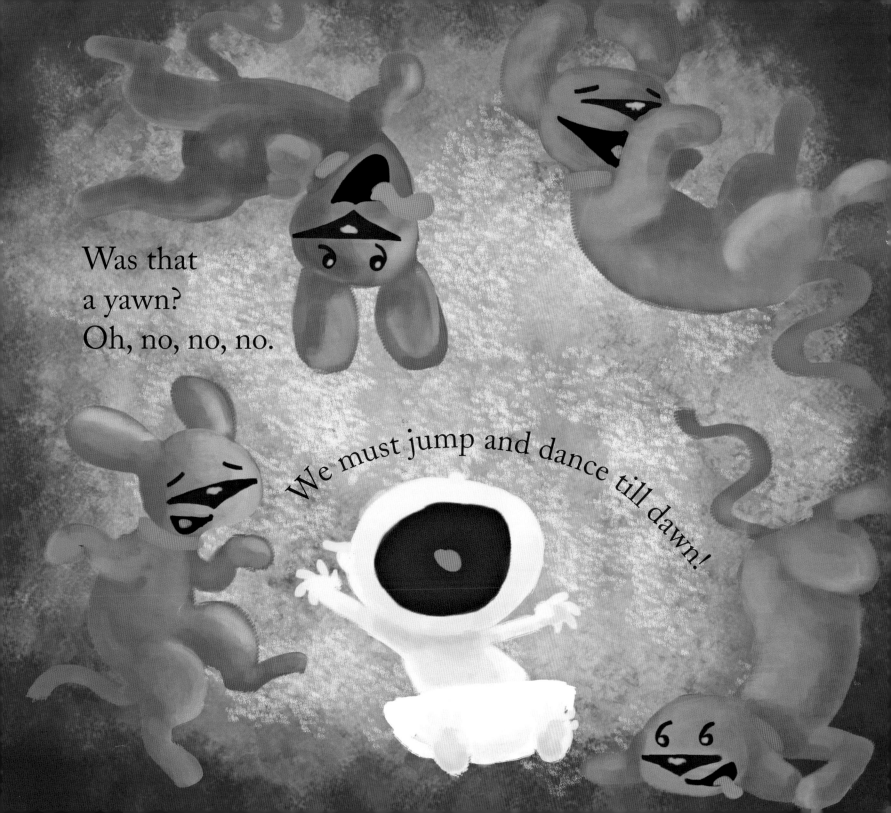

Was that
a yawn?
Oh, no, no, no.

We must jump and dance till dawn!

I hear Mom!
Quick! Under the bed!

Are you snoozing?
Roll around and shake your head!

Get a running start. Don't miss a beat.

Jump under the cool, soft sheets.

Now it's time for nighty night.
Now's the time for counting sheep.

Now it's time for sleepy sleeps.